P9-BJD-635

ORDINARY MIRACLES

"Read ORDINARY MIRACLES aloud and hear a beautiful woman's voice, haunting and intimate, as Erica Jong distills the essence of her life in these new poems." —Nancy Friday

"I was much moved, elated, awed by these new poems. Here is an incredibly honest art."—Anthony Burgess

"Flashing with love, sex, birth, laughter, wisdom and, above all, death, ORDINARY MIRACLES confronts us with the elemental—the walking shadow, the blue transience of existence, itself."—Alvin Toffler

**WHAT CRITICS AND WRITERS HAVE TO SAY
ABOUT ERICA JONG'S POETRY**

"BEGUILING, IMAGINATIVE, INTELLIGENT, THOUGHT-PROVOKING."—*Saturday Review*

"I read these poems the way you watch a trapeze act, with held breath, marvelling at the agility, the lightness of touch, the brilliant demonstration of the difficult made to look easy."—Margaret Atwood

"Erica Jong is a poet who owes nothing to anyone. . . . Compounded of surprises, they are sly but penetrating, witty but passionate, bawdy and beautiful. It is poetry to fall in love with."—Louis Untermeyer

"These are poems made . . . under a star that dances. Witty, sly, provocative and full of fresh and vivid imagery."
—Marge Piercy

"ORIGINAL, SEDUCTIVE, MARVELOUS, POWERFUL!"
—*Cosmopolitan*

BY ERICA JONG

Fruits & Vegetables
(poetry, 1971)

Half-Lives
(poetry, 1973)

Fear of Flying
(fiction, 1973)

Loveroot
(poetry, 1975)

How to Save Your Own Life
(fiction, 1977)

At the Edge of the Body
(poetry, 1979)

Fanny: Being the True History of the
Adventures of Fanny Hackabout-Jones
(fiction, 1980)

Witches
(nonfiction, poetry, 1981)

Ordinary Miracles
(poetry, 1983)

ORDINARY MIRACLES

NEW POEMS BY
ERICA JONG

A PLUME BOOK
NEW AMERICAN LIBRARY
TIMES MIRROR
NEW YORK AND SCARBOROUGH, ONTARIO

NAL BOOKS ARE AVAILABLE AT QUANTITY DISCOUNTS WHEN USED TO
PROMOTE·PRODUCTS OR SERVICES. FOR INFORMATION PLEASE WRITE TO
PREMIUM MARKETING DIVISION, THE NEW AMERICAN LIBRARY, INC.,
1633 BROADWAY, NEW YORK, NEW YORK 10019.

Copyright © 1983 by Erica Mann Jong

All rights reserved.

A hardcover edition of this book has been published simultaneously
by The New American Library, Inc.

Acknowledgments

Atwood, Margaret: "One More Garden" from TRUE STORIES. Copyright ©
1981 by Margaret Atwood. Reprinted by permission of Simon & Schuster.

Blake, William: "Eternity," "And his dark secret love," and "The Marriage of
Heaven and Hell" from THE COMPLETE POETRY AND PROSE OF WILLIAM
BLAKE. Newly Revised Edition edited by David V. Erdman. New York:
Anchor Press/Doubleday, 1982.

Colette: EARTHLY PARADISE, edited by Robert Phelps. New York: Farrar,
Straus and Giroux, 1966.

Lennon, John and McCartney, Paul: "Back in the U.S.S.R." Copyright © 1968
Northern Songs Limited. All rights for the U.S.A., Mexico and The Philippines
controlled by MacClen Music, Inc., c/o ATV Music Corp. Used by permission.
All rights reserved.

Miller, Henry: BLACK SPRING. New York: Grove Press, 1963; TROPIC OF
CAPRICORN, New York: Grove Press, 1962.

Neruda, Pablo: "Night on the Island" and "Oblivion" from THE CAPTAIN'S
VERSES. Copyright © 1972 by Pablo Neruda and Donald D. Walsh. Reprinted
by permission of New Directions Publishing Corp. "XIV Every Day You Play"
from PABLO NERUDA SELECTED POEMS edited by Nathaniel Tarn.
Reprinted by permission of Delacorte Press/Seymour Lawrence, 1973.

Pritchett, V. S.: A CAB AT THE DOOR, A MEMOIR. New York: Random
House, 1968.

Pushkin: "Autumn" from THE BRONZE HORSEMAN AND OTHER POEMS,
translated by D. M. Thomas. Translation copyright © 1982 by D. M. Thomas.
Reprinted by permission of Viking Penguin Inc.

Stoppard, Tom: NIGHT AND DAY. Copyright © 1979 by Tom Stoppard.
Reprinted by permission of Grove Press.

 PLUME TRADEMARK REG. U.S. PAT. OFF. AND FOREIGN COUNTRIES
REGISTERED TRADEMARK—MARCA REGISTRADA
HECHO EN WESTFORD, MASS., U.S.A.

SIGNET, SIGNET CLASSIC, MENTOR, PLUME, MERIDIAN and NAL BOOKS
are published *in the United States* by The New American Library, Inc.,
1633 Broadway, New York, New York 10019, *in Canada* by The New
American Library of Canada Limited, 81 Mack Avenue, Scarborough,
Ontario M1L 1M8

Library of Congress Cataloging in Publication Data

Jong, Erica.
    Ordinary miracles.

    I. Title.
PS3560.0'560'7   1983b   811'.54   83-8222
ISBN 0-452-25436-1

First Printing (Plume), September, 1983

1   2   3   4   5   6   7   8   9

PRINTED IN THE UNITED STATES OF AMERICA

This book is for
Molly, Gerri, Chip

All is flux, all is perishable.
The surface of your being is
constantly crumbling; within
however you grow hard as a diamond.
—HENRY MILLER
Tropic of Capricorn

To piss warm and drink cold, as
Trimalchio says, because our
mother the earth is in the
middle, made round like an egg,
and has all good things in
herself, like a honeycomb.
—HENRY MILLER
Black Spring

He who binds to himself a joy
Does the winged life destroy
But he who kisses the joy as it flies
Lives in eternity's sun rise.
—WILLIAM BLAKE

Contents

A Note from the Author

Does anyone want to hear what a poet has to say about writing poems? Sometimes it seems people would rather hear that than read the poems themselves. Poetry has become a sort of stepchild of American letters. Publishers publish it to be charitable; bookstores order only enough copies to seem virtuous; and reviewers review it in groups of three—as if one volume of verse did not have as much blood between the boards as any novel.

The fault is not with the public or the publishers or the bookstores or the reviewers. Long ago—perhaps as long ago as two or three centuries—the novel replaced the epic as the dominant literary form. Ever since then verse has gradually come to seem vestigial—not one of literature's main concerns, but a museum piece to be studied only by specialists. This is unfortunate because, while some good poetry is hermetic and difficult, intelligible only to scholars, not all good poetry *need* be. Whether one writes clearly or obscurely is often not a choice made by the individual poet; one receives one's style from the muse much as one receives one's subject matter. But some good poets are accessible to a potentially large audience—Whitman, Neruda, Lowell, Roethke, Frost, Auden, Amichai, Plath, Hughes, Sexton (to name only a few)—and since poetry is the most accurate idiom in which to contemplate love and death, it is a waste and a shame that it is so neglected in the English-speaking world today.

When I was a college student, obscure poetry, poetry intelligible only to scholars, was so much the rage that I tried desperately to make my poems obscure. It was in vain. My poems kept coming out clear. That has never ceased to be held against them in academic circles. But after a number of books, a writer learns to accept herself. "One does not choose one's subject matter," Flaubert said, "one submits to it." All poets know that they are merely vessels for the muse or the communal unconscious. We are the White Goddess' pencils; she moves our pens along the page.

From the beginning, from my very first collection of verse in 1971 (*Fruits & Vegetables*), my task has been the same: to write out of a naked female consciousness for a culture that has too often presumed the noun "poet" to be of the male gender. My subjects have been consistent too: sex (both in the sense of eros and of creativity) and death. Yeats says that these are the only subjects worthy of the poet's attention, and I suppose he is right. Insofar as poetry is the most passionate and distilled utterance of the human condition, the human dilemma, it must deal with the creative and erotic lusts which drive us and the contemplation of death which stops us short. That these are inextricably allied should come as a surprise to no one. We humans have a relatively short span of years to inhabit our corporeality, and during that span we must push our corporeality to the outer limit in order to intuit what may lie beyond it. If many modern poets have been criticized for an obsession with sex, an obsession with extreme experiences, it should also come as a surprise to no one that that criticism has never deterred them from pursuing these things. Why? Because poets know instinctively that they must live to the limit what other humans merely inhale from afar. They were put on earth to be not merely mortals, but specimen mortals, and they must wallow in their own mortality, which often means wallowing in their own sexuality.

Is it permissible to be a poet and a novelist, too? In America, where writers are frequently asked to choose a major in the great graduate school of life, pursuing two literary genres is sometimes thought promiscuous and dilettantish —suspect at the least. But no less talents than Thomas Hardy and D. H. Lawrence wrote both poems and novels, and outside the English-speaking world, no similar taboo exists about a writer manifesting his destiny in more than one form. Prior to this volume, I have written four books of poetry and three novels (as well as one book which contains both prose and poetry: *Witches*). I find that the volumes of verse tend to predict themes in the novels to come —almost as if I were distilling my life one way in poetic form, and another way in prosaic. The poems are a more intense, more concentrated chronicle. In lyric poems, one cannot really show the fabric of society, nor can one write the sort of social satire that is one of the great delights of novel-writing. But the intensity of utterance more than compensates for this. One can declare love, decry death, howl out the pain of loss. And the human voice activates a poem, gives it new life. When one reads a poem aloud, that moment of existence comes back with as much intensity as it was lived. Sometimes more. The poem is a sort of time capsule in which one traps intense moments of life— epiphanies. If the poem lives, that moment is held in suspension to be released again whenever the text interacts with the human voice. The poem, in short, is as much a container of energy as the unsplit atom. Speaking the poem aloud should activate the energy in much the same way as splitting the atom activates nuclear force. Thinking in terms of this atomic metaphor makes it clear that the poem is far more than a sort of replay of life. It both records mortal moments and reaches beyond mortality. It gazes at the infinite through lids of flesh.

At the moment of completing *Ordinary Miracles*, I am in the midst of writing my fourth novel. In re-reading this collection, I see the novel-in-progress, almost as one sees one's own skeleton through a fluoroscope screen. There are poems about pregnancy, childbirth, parenthood, the pain of divorce, the acceptance of death, the situation of the writer in mid-career, the fear of succumbing to love, and the inevitable renaissance of creativity and hope that comes only when one remains open to loving. My poems and my novels have always been very much of a piece. In *Fruits & Vegetables* (1971) and *Half-Lives* (1973) I see the themes of

Fear of Flying (1973) as if in a crystal ball. *Loveroot* (1975) predicts many of the preoccupations of *How to Save Your Own Life* (1977); and *At the Edge of the Body* (1979) anticipates the concern with the metaphysical which found expression in *Fanny: Being the True History of the Adventures of Fanny Hackabout-Jones* (1980) and *Witches* (1981). I am always hoping that someone will recognize the poet and novelist as two aspects of the same soul—but alas, the genres are reviewed by two different groups of people, so no one ever seems to notice this in print. What matter? I have the best of it—the joy of writing itself.

T. S. Eliot once said that a poet is someone who keeps writing poems after his thirtieth birthday, and by this measure I have made it, though it was direly predicted by many detractors that I would give up poetry after the success of *Fear of Flying.* I keep on writing poems because poetry is the wellspring of all my other work, and also because there is no more ecstatic experience than receiving a first line from above and spinning it, weaving it, dreaming it, into a poem. After writing a poem, I skip about the house like my four-year-old daughter; I sing; I want to read it aloud to all the world. A poem is a sort of miracle given to one by the muse. It is a gift, while the novel is earned, page by interminable page. One labors hard at the novel so that the reader may play. One crawls so the reader may fly. Novel-writing is, in short, like mining salt. Poem-writing is like flying.

Who would give up that delirious flight once having experienced it? It would be like giving up life, like giving up sex, like giving up the joy of loving and being loved. Poetry is my pleasure, my reward, the most blissful experience of my literary life. Or of my life. Let's just say that: of my life.

ERICA JONG

Weston, Connecticut
January 1983

ORDINARY
MIRACLES

FETAL HEARTBEAT

We were born & what
happened before that
is myth.
—V. S. PRITCHETT

*Il faut de la merde
pour pousser les roses.*
—FRENCH PROVERB

Ordinary Miracles

Spring, rainbows,
ordinary miracles
about which
nothing new can be said.

The stars on a clear night
of a New England winter;
the soft air of the islands
along the old
Spanish Main;
pirate gold shining
in the palm;
the odor of roses
to the lover's nose . . .

There is no more poetry
to be written
of these things.
The rainbow's sudden revelation—
behold!
the cliché is true!
What can one say
but that?

So too
with you, little heart,
little miracle,

but you are
no less miracle
for being
ordinary.

The Birth of the Water Baby

Little egg,
little nub,
full complement of
fingers, toes,
little rose blooming
in a red universe,
which once wanted you less
than emptiness,
but now holds you
fast,
containing your rapid heart
beat under its
slower one
as the earth
contains the sea . . .

Oh avocado pit
almost ready to sprout,
tiny fruit tree
within sight
of the sea,
little swimming fish,
little land lover,
hold on!
hold on!

Here, under my heart
you'll keep
till it's time
for us to meet,
& we come apart
that we may come

together,
& you are born
remembering
the wavesound
of my blood,
the thunder of my heart,
& like your mother
always dreaming
of the sea.

Another Language

The whole world is flat
& I am round.
Even women avert their eyes,
& men, embarrassed
by the messy way
that life turns into life,
look away,
forgetting they themselves
were once this roundness
underneath the heart,
this helpless fish
swimming in eternity.

The sound of O,
not the sound of I
embarrasses the world.
My friends, who voluntarily have made
their bodies flat,
their writings flat as grief,
look at me in disbelief.
What is this large unseemly thing—
a pregnant poet?
an enormous walking O?
Oh take all letters of the alphabet but that!
We speak the Esperanto of the flat!

Condemned to sign
language & silence, pregnant poems
for men to snicker at,
for women to denounce,
I live alone.
My world is round

& bounded by the mountain of my fear;
while all the great geographers agree
the world is flat
& roundness cannot be.

Anti-Conception

Could I unthink you,
little heart,
what would I do?
Throw you out
with last night's garbage,
undo my own decisions,
my own flesh
& commit you to the void
again?

Fortunately,
it is not my problem.
You hold on, beating
like a little clock,
Swiss in your precision,
Japanese in your tenacity,
& already having
your own karma,

while I, with my half-
hearted maternal urges,
my uncertainty that any creature
ever really creates
another (unless it be
herself) know you
as God's poem
& myself merely as publisher,
as midwife,
as impresario,
oh, even, if you will,
as loathèd producer
of your *Grand Spectacle:*

you are the star,
& like your humblest fan,
I wonder
(gazing at your image
on the screen)
who you really are.

Perishable Women

Perishable women—
the colonial graveyards
are strewn with your bones,
the islands of the Caribbean
are rich with your deaths.
You perished
like the creatures of the reefs,
bringing forth your kind.

Perishable women—
dying at twenty, twenty-three,
"Beloved wife & Tender Mother,"
long lamented by your husband
(& his wives),
survivors who outlasted you,
then died
the way you died.

Only the men lived on
to perish in the wars,
to die of sharkbite
or of fever, bloody flux,
the smallpox, even leprosy
or gout
(one ate well
on these islands in the sun).

Everyone was perishable;
children died
like flies;
& women died
in giving birth to children
who would die.

God was blamed,
& Nature's mighty hand
which wrought her handiwork
imperfectly,
& broke a hundred vessels
in the sea
that one whole
cup might be.

Perishable women—
smashed like pots
upon the floor beneath the wheel,
crushed like shells upon the beach,
like husks of coconut,
like bits of bottle glass.

At my age I'd be dead.

You would not be.

Birthdays

Next birthday
I am thirty-six,
& formed (for all intents
& purposes)
in tooth & claw.
Six books
have peeled away
all that I am
& all
that I am not;
I turn back pages now
in history's dog-eared
book, & write
of other lives.

& here you come,
pink as dawn,
rosy as the aurora borealis
blooming over Yorkshire
& the ruined abbeys
of the Lake District,
curly as a baby sheep,
hungry as a little billy
goat, cuddly
as a lap dog,
able to flex your spine
to fit inside my own,
& born
between piss
& shit.

I welcome you
with all my breath

& guts;
I hallelujah
to your eyes, your heart,
your tender toes.
May I keep growing younger
with your years
until, when you are just my age,
or more, I have gone back to zero
& am ready,
perhaps then,
to be reborn.

Anti-Matter

I am not interested
in my body—
the part that stinks
& rots & brings forth
life,
the part that the ground
swallows,
death giving birth
to death—
all of life,
considered
from the body's
point of view,
is a downhill slide
& all our small
preservatives
& griefs
cannot reverse the trend.

All sensualists
turn puritan
at the end—
turning up lust's soil
& finding bones
beneath the rich volcanic
dirt.

Some sleep in shrouds
& some in coffins;
some swear off
procreation, others turn
vegetarian, or worse:

they live on air—
on sheer platonic meals
of pure ideas;
once gluttons of the flesh,
they now become
gourmets of the mind.

How to resist that
when the spacious earth
swallows her children
so insatiably,
when all our space-age gods
are grounded,
& only the moan of pleasure
or the rasp of pain
can ever satisfy
the body's appetite?

& yet my body,
in its dubious wisdom,
led to yours;
& you may
puzzle out
this mystery in your turn.
Choose mind, choose body,
choose to wed the two;
many have tried
but few have done the deed.

Through you, perhaps,
I may at last succeed.

The Protection We Bear

Pregnant, we know god,
this presence inside us
which protects us
yet makes us
vulnerable.

My baby
flowed out around me
protecting me
in her own radiance
for nine whole months.

I was never alone.
I did not fear death.
The baby within
& the spirit without
were one,
& I was at peace.

Then she was born,
& fear reclaimed me.

Erica, Erica,
don't you know
that if you can create
a baby, you can also create god?
& if god can bloom
a baby in your belly
then She
must be
with you always?

On the First Night

On the first night
of the full moon,
the primeval sack of ocean
broke,
& I gave birth to you
little woman,
little carrot top,
little turned-up nose,
pushing you out of myself
as my mother
pushed
me out of herself,
as her mother did,
& her mother's mother before her,
all of us born
of woman.

I am the second daughter
of a second daughter
of a second daughter,
but you shall be the first.
You shall see the phrase
"second sex"
only in puzzlement,
wondering how anyone,
except a madman,
could call you "second"
when you are so splendidly
first,
conferring even on your mother
firstness, vastness, fullness
as the moon at its fullest
lights up the sky.

Now the moon is full again
& you are four weeks old.
Little lion, lioness,
yowling for my breasts,
growling at the moon,
how I love your lustiness,
your red face demanding,
your hungry mouth howling,
your screams, your cries
which all spell life
in large letters
the color of blood.

You are born a woman
for the sheer glory of it,
little redhead, beautiful screamer.
You are no second sex,
but the first of the first;
& when the moon's phases
fill out the cycle
of your life,
you will crow
for the joy
of being a woman,
telling the pallid moon
to go drown herself
in the blue ocean,
& glorying, glorying, glorying
in the rosy wonder
of your sunshining wondrous
self.

For Molly
(A Verbal Cuddle for an Eight-month-old)

You—the purest pleasure
of my life,
the split pit
that proves
the ripeness of the fruit,
the unbroken center
of my broken hopes—

O little one,
making you
has centered my lopsided life

so that if I know
a happiness
that reason never taught,
it is because of your small
unreasonably wrigglish
limbs.
Daughter, little bean,
sprout, sproutlet, smallest
girleen,
just saying your name
makes me grin.

I used to hate the word Mother,
found it obscene,
& now I love it
since that is me
to you.

For Molly, Concerning God

Is God the one who eats the meat
off the bones of dead people?
—Molly Miranda Jong-Fast, age 3½.

God is the one,
Molly,
whether we call him
Him,
or Her,
treeform or spewing
volcano,
Vesuvius or vulva,
penis-rock,
or reindeer-on-cave-wall,
God is the one
who eats
our meat,
Molly,
& we yield
our meat
up willingly.

Meat is our
element,
meat is our
lesson.

When our bodies fill
with each other,
when our blood swells
in our organs
aching for another,
body of meat,

heart of meat,
soul of meat,
we are only doing
what God wants
us to—
meat joining meat
to become insubstantial air,
meat fusing
with meat
to make
a small wonder
like you.

The wonder of you
is that you push
our questions
along into
the future—
so that I know
again
the wonder of meat
through you,
the wonder of meat
turning to philosophy,
the wonder of meat
transubstantiated
into poetry,
the wonder of
sky-blue meat
in your roundest eyes,
the wonder of
dawn-colored meat
in your cheeks & palms,
the wonder of meat
becoming
air.

You
are my theorem,
my proof,
my meaty metaphysics,
my little questioner,
my small Socrates
of the nursery-schoolyard.

To think that
such wonder
can come from meat!

Well then,
if God is hungry—
let Him eat,
let Her eat.

Poem for Molly's Fortieth Birthday

"Why do you
have stripes
in your forehead,
Mama?
Are you
old?"

Not old.
But not so
young
that I cannot
see
the world contracting
upon itself
& the circle
closing
at the end.

As the furrows
in my brow
deepen,
I can see
myself
sinking back
into that childhood
street
I walked along
with my grandfather,
thinking *he* was old
at sixty-three
since I was four,
as you are four

to my
forty.

Forty years
to take
the road out . . .
Will another forty
take me
back?

Back to the street
I grew up on,
back to
my mother's breast,
back to the second
world war
of a second
child,
back
to the cradle
endlessly
rocking?

I am young
as *you* are,
Molly—
yet with stripes
in my brow;
I earn my youth
as you must earn
your age.

These stripes
are decorations
for my valor—
forty years

of marching
to a war
I could not
declare,
nor locate,
yet have somehow
won.

Now,
I begin
to unwin,
unravelling
the sleeves
of care
that have
stitched up
this brow,
unravelling
the threads
that have kept
me scared,
as I pranced
over the world,
seemingly fearless,
working
without a net,
knowing
if I fell
it would
only be
into that same
childhood street,
where I dreaded
to tread
on the lines—
not knowing

the lines
would someday
tread
on me.

Molly,
when you are forty,
read this poem
& tell me:
have we won
or lost
the war?

II

THE BREATH INSIDE THE BREATH

One must act as if the next
step were the last, which it is.
Each step forward is the last, and
with it a world dies, oneself included.
We are here of the earth never to end,
the past never ceasing, the future never
beginning, the present never ending.
—HENRY MILLER
Black Spring

The Horse from Hell

(Elegy for My Grandfather
Who Painted the Sea & Horses)

A dream of fantastic horses
galloping out of the sea,
the sea itself a dream,
a dream of green on green,
an age of indolence
where one-celled animals
blossom, once more, into limbs,
brains, pounding hooves,
out of the terrible innocence
of the waves.

Venice on the crest
of hell's typhoon,
sunami of my dreams
when, all at once,
I wake at three a.m.
in a tidal wave of love & sleeplessness,
anxiety & dread . . .

Up from the dream,
up on the shining white
ledge of dread—
I dredge the deep
for proof that we do not die,
for proof that love
is a seawall against despair,
& find only
the one-celled dreams
dividing & dividing
as in the primal light.

O my grandfather,
you who painted the sea
so obsessively,
you who painted horses
galloping, galloping
out of the sea—
go now,
ride on the bare back
of the unsaddled,
unsaddleable horse
who would take you
straight to hell.

Gallop on the back
of all my nightmares;
dance in the foam
in a riot of hooves
& let the devil paint you
with his sea-green brush;
let him take you
into the waves at last,
until you fall,
chiming forever,
through the seaweed bells,
lost like the horses of San Marco,
but not for good.

Down through the hulls
of gelatinous fish,
down through the foamless foam
which coats your bones,
down through the undersea green
which changes your flesh
into pure pigment,
grinding your eyes down
to the essential cobalt blue.

Let the bones of my poems
support what is left of you—
ashes & nightmares,
canvasses half-finished & fading worksheets.

O my grandfather,
as you die,
a poem forms on my lips,
as foam forms
on the ocean's morning mouth,
& I sing in honor of the sea & you—

the sea who defies all paintings
& all poems
& you
who defy
the sea.

On Reading a Vast Anthology

Love, death, sleeping
with somebody else's husband
or wife—this
is what poetry is
about—Eskimo, Aztec,
or even Italian
Rinascimento,
or even the high falutin Greeks
or noble Roman-O's.

O the constant turmoil
of the human species—
beds, graves, Spring with its
familiar rosebuds, the wrong beds,
the wrong graves, wars
unremembered & boundaries gained
only to be lost & lost
again
& lost roses whose lost
petals
reminded poets to *carpe, carpe*
diem with whoever's wife
or husband happened to
be handiest!

O Turmoil & Confusion—
you are my Muses!
O longing for a world
without death, without beds
divided by walls between houses!
All the beds float out to sea!
All the dying lovers wave

to the other dying lovers!
One of them writes on his mistress's skin as he floats.

He is the poet.
Not for this
will his life be spared.

The Poet as a Feeler of Pain

What makes a poet?
Many have tried to guess.
Is it a voice
like a conduit,
a plainspokenness to grief,
the hairs of the head
dancing on end,
the blood swarming
with the voices
of all those who have died,
will die,
& will also be born?

Is it a catch
in the throat
that awakens the eyes,
is it in the eyes themselves
or is it something
in the heart?

I think it is pain—
an openness to pain,
so that the least leaf
cuts the hand
& the smallest tear
cuts the cheek
like jagged crystal,

so that the world
is a sick infant
& the poet its mother,
praying, crooning, promising
to be good

if only the cure
takes.

There is, of course,
no cure.

Poetry does not cure
the poet
& the poet
does not cure
the world.

Usually he catches
the world's diseases
& dies
even before his time.

But against all odds
& all indifference,
another one is born.
The world must have
someone to feel its pain
& speak of it.

The poet is that mouth.

The Cover of the Book

The cover of the book
is astral violet,
& within it
are poems,
most of them
earthbound,
but for one
to the poet's
daughter
which soars
into
the empyrean
on umbilical wings.

Oh we poets
are so afraid
of making babies—
& yet
of all
the fleshly chains
that bind us,
our children
are the chains
that bind
most closely
to heaven.

How can that be?

Poetry
is an astral
affliction.

Poets are always
saving themselves
for their poems.
Yet in that saving
there is no grace,
while in the child
there is distraction,
chaos, disorder

& through that fleshly chaos

peace.

The Poet Fears Failure

The poet fears failure
& so she says
"Hold on pen—
what if the critics
hate me?"
& with that question
she blots out more lines
than any critic could.

The critic is only doing his job:
keeping the poet lonely.
He barks
like a dog at the door
when the master comes home.

It's in his doggy nature.
If he didn't know the poet
for the boss,
he wouldn't bark so loud.

& the poet?
It's in her nature
to fear failure
but not to let that fear
blot out

her lines.

This Element

Looking for a place
where we might turn off
the inner dialogue,
the monologue
of futures & regrets,
of pasts not past enough
& futures that may never come
to pass,
we found this boat
bobbing in the blue,
this refuge amid reefs,
this white hull
within this azure sibilance of sea,
this central rocking
so like the rocking
before birth.

Venus was born of the waters,
borne over them
to teach us about love—
our only sail
on the seas of our lives
as death is
our only anchor.

If we return again & again
to the sea
both in our dreams
& for our love affairs
it is because
this element alone

understands our pasts
& futures
as she makes them

one.

On the Avenue

Male?
Female?
God doesn't care
about sex
& the long tree-shaded avenue
toward death.

God says
the worm is as beautiful
as the apple it eats
& the apple as lovely
as the thick trunk
of the tree,
& the trunk of the tree
no more beautiful
than the air
surrounding it.

God doesn't care
about the battle
between the sexes
with which we amuse ourselves
on our way toward death.

God says:
there are no sexes;
& still we amuse ourselves
arguing about whether or not
She is male
or He

female.

The Central Passion

What is the central passion
of a life?
To please mummy & daddy?
To find a home for their furniture?
To found a family of one's own,
possibly a dynasty?
To fill the world with more books
that have no readers
or books that have too many
& kill
too many trees?

What is the passion
that drives us
as the wind drives
a winged seed?
To reproduce ourselves,
then die?
To meet God once
if only in a dream?
To reach enlightenment
through pain
or pleasure?

Or perhaps just
to question
as I am doing now,
& to teach by questioning . . .

Yes—this is both passion
& power
enough.

What You Need to Be a Writer
For Ben

After the college
reading,
the eager
students gather.

They ask me
what you need
to be a writer

& I, feeling flippant,
jaunty
(because
I am wearing
an 18th century
dress
& think
myself in love
again),
answer:

"*Mazel*,
determination,
talent,
& true
grit."

I even
believe it—

looking
as I do
like an

advertisement
for easy
success—

designer dress,
sly smile
on my lips
& silver boots
from
Oz.

Suppose
they saw me
my eyes
swollen
like sponges,
my hand
shaking
with betrayal,

my fear
rampant
in the dark?

Suppose they saw
the fear
of never
writing,
the fear
of being
alone,
the money fear,
the fear fear,
the fear
of succumbing
to fear?

& then
there's all
I did
not say:

to be
a writer
what you need
is

something
to say:

something
that burns
like a hot coal
in your gut

something
that pounds
like a pump
in your groin

& the courage
to live
like a wound

that never
heals.

Poem to Kabir

Kabir says
the breath inside the breath
is God

& I say to Kabir
you are the breath inside that breath
which is not to say
that the poet is God—

but only that God
uses the poet
as the wind
uses
a sail.

III

THE HEART, THE CHILD, THE WORLD

bread, wine, love, and anger—
I heap upon you
because you are the cup
that was waiting for the gifts of my life.
—NERUDA

O reason not the need!
—SHAKESPEARE
King Lear

To Jon in October

Knowing our lives a drowse
towards death
(attended by dogs
& children)
how can it not matter
that I remember
(day after day)
that one day
we shall lose
each other,
lose the lights
in each other's eyes
to death,
& drift off
to other universes.

Love shall not save us
from being alone at the end,
& the daughter we made
in that fine high exuberance
of having found each other
shall not save us either.

We shall go off
into the ether alone,
trying to remember
(as the threads unravel
& the brain cells turn
to fluffy cumulus clouds)

that on clear October days
like this one,
when the hills were

red with maple,
gold with oak,
we bumped along in the Jeep
reminding each other:
"Wake up! Wake up!
This will not last forever!"

Time Leak

For centuries
we have lain like this,
our warmths intermingled,
our hearts beating
the same two-step,
& our breaths
& our limbs
intertwined.

Life after life,
I return to flesh
to join my flesh
to your flesh.
Sometimes I am the woman
& you the man;
sometimes,
the other way around.

It hardly matters.
Flesh after flesh,
our spirits return
to mingle.
Death is no barrier
& life's noisy matinee
where the suburban ladies
cough & sputter
& their programs crackle like kindling
merely goes on & on.

They sit on their deaths
as if they were sitting

on fur coats,
while we touch
for the first time
remembering
the next.

The Heart, the Child, the World

Out in the world, the child
cries for the mother
as the wound cries for salt
as the lover cries
for her unrequited lover
as the ice cries out
for melting in the spring.

My heart is a spring
that pumps red blood.
I would give my child,
my girl child, my daughter
the vision of a mother
who does not flinch
when the heavy heel of man
comes down,
who loves the penis
when it pumps rich red blood
but values the wholeness
of her heart
above that battering organ,
that dumb implement,
which can so easily turn
from kind to cruel.

My heart is out in the world
like an orphan howling
on a street corner.
I want a warm, safe place
to hide with my books, my child,
my heart
that is scarred,
seamed like a belly

which has given birth
to an imperious baby Caesar

but still,
despite its bursting fullness,

whole.

Letter to My Lover After Seven Years

You gave me the child
that seamed my belly
& stitched up my life.

You gave me: one book of love poems,
five years of peace
& two of pain.

You gave me darkness, light, laughter
& the certain knowledge
that we someday die.

You gave me seven years
during which the cells of my body
died & were reborn.

Now we have died
into the limbo of lost loves,
that wreckage of memories
tarnishing with time,
that litany of losses
which grows longer with the years,
as more of our friends
descend underground
& the list of our loved dead
outstrips the list of the living.

Knowing as we do
our certain doom,
knowing as we do
the rarity of the gifts we gave
& received,
can we redeem

our love from that limbo,
dust it off like a fine sea trunk
found in an attic
& now more valuable
for its age & rarity
than a shining new one?

Probably not.
This page is spattered
with tears that streak the words
lost, losses, limbo.

I stand on a ledge in hell
still howling for our love.

If You Come Back

If you come back
now
before the roadblocks
are too many,
before too many bodies
are stacked
between us,
before the demilitarized zone
fills up with the mud
of betrayal,
& counter-betrayal,
we may still find
it in our hearts
to trust each other.
We may still find
it in our bodies
to fit together.
We may still find
that our minds
curl around the same
jokes and rejoice
in the same
hijinks.

But if we wait
till the bodies pile up
to the sky,
till the blood
dries in the muddy trench,
we may just find
that it turns
to pale powder
& blows away.

For we know that
love can dry up
as surely as arroyos
were once raging rivers,
as surely as swamps
are deserts now,
as surely as oceans
turn to sand.

I do not fear
the blood
as much as I fear
its drying
until the smallest breath
can blow
our love, our dreams,
our mingled flesh

away.

There Is Only One Story

There is only one story:
he loved her,
then stopped loving her,
while she did not
stop loving him.

There is only one story:
she loved him,
then stopped loving him,
while he did not
stop loving her.

The truth is simple:
you do not die
from love.

You only wish
you did.

You Hate the Telephone

You hate the telephone
but will not see me
face to face
so I am left
beseeching you
long-distance,
trying to thread our love
along the telephone poles
of Vermont,
trying to tunnel it
under the Atlantic
as if it were
a rare fossil
I'd unearthed,
or an offshore pipe
bearing precious oil.

But it is your face
I love,
your funny grin
that now seems
cruel around the edges.
You do not wish to be
cruel—you,
the kindest person in the world,
but driven to curious
rages
when you feel
pressured, frustrated,
saddled with
an albatross of love
like an ancient
mariner

who tells his same sad story
to the wedding guests.

The telephone will not
suffice.
Coleridge would have
loathed it,
& so would his
mariner.
It is our modern
Person from Porlock,
interrupting poems,
interrupting loves
& forever
keeping us at arm's length.

I would look you in the eye
again, saying yes, yes, yes—
we have said *no* enough,
for the rest
of many lifetimes.

My Love Is Too Much

My love is too much—
it embarrasses you—
blood, poems, babies,
red needs that telephone
from foreign countries,
black needs that spatter
the pages
of your white papery heart.

You would rather have a girl
with simpler needs:
lunch, sex, undemanding
loving,
dinner, wine, bed,
the occasional blow-job
& needs that are never
red as gaping wounds
but cool & blue
as television screens
in tract houses.

Oh my love,
those simple girls
with simple needs
read my books too.

They tell me they feel
the same as I do.

They tell me I transcribe
the language of their hearts.
They tell me I translate
their mute, unspoken pain

into the white light
of language.

Oh love,
no love
is ever wholly undemanding.
It can pretend coolness
until the pain comes,
until the first baby comes,
howling her own infant need
into a universe
that never summoned her.

The love you seek
cannot be found
except in the white pages
of recipe books.

It is cooking you seek,
not love,
cooking with sex coming after,
cool sex
that speaks to the penis alone,
& not the howling chaos
of the heart.

Two Bubble-Headed Lovers
(or, *The Zipless Fuck, reconsidered*)

Two bubble-headed lovers
joined by a spring
clasp each other on my desk.
He has his arms propped up
& his legs together.
She has her legs spread wide
& her arms crossed coolly under her head.

If I squeeze their lucite legs,
he seems to pump against her thighs,
(though he has no penis)
& she, in her transparent plastic passion,
coldly receives him
(though she has no cunt).

It is only a toy,
a silly lucite gewgaw,
a glorified paperclip
bought at a glorified
paperclip store.

But he has an air bubble
where his heart should be
& she has a larger one
where her womb would be,
& no matter how many poems
I clasp between their empty heads
their lovemaking will never change
until the plastic melts,
or they both are

broken.

Imagining You with Another Woman

Imagining you
with another woman.
Your imperious penis
probing the cosmos
between her legs.
I should not care,
it is not modern to care
knowing that my caring
only makes you feel guilty
& that if I say go ahead
you feel neglected
& if I say *stop*
you feel
I am giving
you guilt.

Go ahead.
I swallow back
the curdled love
that rises like vomit.
I hold back the tears
that spring in my eyes
like that silent spring
which filled where a virgin
was raped
& died.

Even if you do not care
whom I take between my legs
or whom I love.
Even if you are cool, modern,
turned on by tales of lust

casual & strong,
I am not you.

When I imagine you
with another woman
the pain seals off my heart
as if with scar tissue;
the pain stops
the spring of my love
as if a drought had come
& dried up all the rivers;
the pain eats up the love.

I try to hold onto the love
knowing that sex,
after all, can be casual,
foolish, no great matter,
but as long as I love you
I am open
to pain so terrible
it blocks my life, my writing,
the very sun of my being.

I would be cool.
I would be modern.
I would rather not love
than feel such pain.

Because I Would Not Admit

And his dark secret love
Does thy life destroy.
—WILLIAM BLAKE

Because I would not admit
that I had nurtured
an enemy within my breast—

a lover who wanted to gnaw
my secret rose,
a lover who wanted to press me
between the covers of a book,
then burn it,
a lover-usurper who wanted
to take my soul—

I nearly died,
running my car upon rocks
like a badly steered sloop,
crashing into trees
like a hurricane gale,
burning my arms in ovens
(when I thought I was only
baking bread). . . .

To admit the betrayal
was worse than
the fact of betrayal—
for I loved him
as leaves love sun,
turning my face to him,
turning my hips, my womb
to be filled with a dream

of children, a dream of books
& babies sprouting like leaves
from a spring tree,
a dream of trees that leaked blood
instead of sap. . . .

The dream's the thing—
the dream we die for,
turning our faces to the sun,
eyes closed, never seeing it has
gone out:
dead star, it blazes coldly
over a dead planet
while we bask in its afterglow,
now remembered in the mind.

He was fond
of stars & telescopes;
fond of machines, fond
of building the most complex
contraptions
to scale the clouds.
But Icarus flies
near the sun with waxen wings,
& does not think of gears
or motors.

Trees rise up at him
as he falls; the earth
rushes to meet him
like a lover
raising her writhing hips;
the wings weep their waxy tears
& fall apart;
the sun is hot
on his face.

But even as he falls
he is in ecstasy;
his sun has not
gone out.

Hotel Rooms

Hotel rooms constitute a separate
moral universe.
—TOM STOPPARD

A bed, a telephone, the cord
to the world
beyond the womb. . . .
Here lovers meet, have met,
will meet again behind different faces
while the icy pictures
look on,
seeing nothing.

Hotel rooms see nothing.

Business transacted,
prostitutes killed,
marriages silently shaken;
what happens here
is off the record;
there is no record
when the sheets
are changed
every night
for other guests.

& you my darling
my lover, my reader,
ultimately
myself,
why are you hungering so,
why are you opening
abysses in yourself

before you rush off
to the next appointment?

Eternity is just
a hotel room—
deluxe or seedy
as the fates allow,
lonely as the loneliest
one-night stand,
& with no telephone.

Or is it the body?
Is the body
the hotel room after all?
O let us inhabit it amply, crying
& screaming & embracing
before we

check out.

To Whom It May Concern

In Autumn,
as in Spring,
the sap flows,
the sap wishes to race
against heartbeats
before the winter,
before the winter
buries us
in her usual shroud of ice.

I turn to you
knowing that
unrequited love
is good
for poetry,
knowing that pain
will nudge the muse
as well as anything,
knowing that you
are afraid, fettered
to a life
you do not love,
& so unfree
that freedom seems
more fearful even
than the familiar
business
of being
a grumbling slave.

I lived
that way
once,

& I know
that freedom
is its own reward,
that it propagates
itself
by means
of runners,

that nobody
gives it to you,
not even me
to you,

but that you
must seize it
with your own
two quaking hands
& pluck
the strawberry
it bears
in the green
ungrumbling

Spring.

IV

STRAW IN THE FIRE

I want to do with you
what Spring does with
the cherry trees.
—NERUDA

Your heart is all ears.
—COLETTE

Bloodsong

In love you have loosened
yourself like seawater. . . .
—NERUDA

You,
loosened by blood,
the blood coursing
in & out of your body,
your body broken
on the wheel
of your own passion,
your own rage to live
so potent
you would die
for it,
your own tears
so salty
they would swell your lids
like rain clouds.

You,
broken on the wheel
of my body,
your cock plowing
through blood,
the sheets
mad with it,
& me crying aloud
for you to break me
& break me again,
wanting that brokenness
in order to heal

& be whole,
wanting that strange stigmata
which ringed your lips,
your cock,
the night you drove
off the snowy road
& into my blood.

You,
saying your veins
were full of me,
as if I were your transfusion,
& you still lay
dying,
the tubes weaving
in & out of your body
& your spleen burst
& your gut
shattered as if by shrapnel.

You,
with the scars
up & down your body,
with a smile
on your lips
& ground glass
in your gut,
with anger so deep
it makes you
drive nails in your palms,
& pain so deep
not even your jokes
can keep it
at bay.

You,
plowing through blood
into snow,
through snow
into blood.
You drove off
my road
& into my blood,
ready to spill your own
to be
muse for a day,
temporary Adonis,
pale angel
whose aura
is blood,
& whose golden nimbus
lights up
my winter
sky.

A Question Mark

There is a hinge
of bone
where your chin joins
your cheek.
I like to stroke it
in the flicker
of a local movie;

I like to take
your laborer's hand
when you are
cautiously—
(O proof of love!)—
driving my car.

You bring me gifts
of food;
I write you
poems of blood.

Your scars are vertical;
mine are horizontal.

You lost your spleen;
I loosed a daughter
on the world.

Your hinge of bone
tells jokes;
while mine chants
poems.

An unlikely pair,
though which pair
is ever likely?

When I cannot
look at your face,
I look
at your cock—
a question mark
asking the sky

how can
heaven
be fucked?

Flying at Forty

You call me
courageous,
I who grew up
gnawing on books,
as some kids
gnaw
on bubble gum,

who married disastrously
not once
but three times,
yet have a lovely daughter
I would not undo
for all the dope
in California.

Fear was my element,
fear my contagion.
I swam in it
till I became
immune.
The plane takes off
& I laugh aloud.
Call me courageous.

I am still alive.

Some I Have Loved

Some I loved
because they were
like me,
& some
because they were
different—
but always
one sees
in a lover
a mirror:

You I love
because you are
scarred like me
& because like me
you will
never grow old.

Mine is
a curious fate:
to remake myself
every seven years,
to shed my skin—
both snake
& Lilith—
& then disappear
from my life.

Lovers have come
& gone.
Through them
I have loved—
What?—

Love itself?
Life? Impermanence?
The unappeasable lover
in myself?

Or is it the poet—
the poet needing
to be in love
as the river
needs rain
in order to flow?

O I shall
flood my banks
for you—
my blue-eyed
river god,
my wheat-colored
harvest,
flood-tide, seed & semen
in which I swim.

Only when we
are parted
shall I wonder
whether I loved
you yourself

or through you,
Love—
whoever
he may be.

The Rose

You gave me a rose
last time we met.

I told myself
if it bloomed
our love would bloom,
& if it died—

O I did not
consider
the possibility.

It died.

Though I cut
the stem
on a slant
as my mother
taught me,
though I dropped
an aspirin
in the water,

it hung its head
like a spent cock
& died.

It stands
on my desk now—
straight green stalk,
blood-red clot
of bud
drooping

like a hanged man's
head.

Does this mean
we are doomed?
Does this mean
all lovers
are doomed?

O my love—
I have not read roses
as amulets
in seven years. . . .

Which doom
is worse?
To love
& lose?

Or to lose
love
altogether
& not care
whether roses

live or die?

Last Flash

Sometimes I think
of how you are hardly
alive,
of how we are all
hardly
alive,

dodging bullets,
dodging raindrops,
skidding on the ice
of Connecticut
winters,
narrowly missing
death
by botulism,
death in its
rattling can,
death by jaw,
death by womb, by cock,
death by
telepathy.

When I think of
your nuclear dreams
& the way you fuck—
head turned sideways
as if you saw
the Last Flash
(& were shielding
your eyes
with me)—
I think
that we are all

marked
beyond repair
by the notion
that even death
can die,

& that our children
will not know
the unutterable joy
of burying
their parents.

I bury you.
You bury me.
Our ages do not
matter—
since I am
life to you,
love, mother,
aunt & anodyne,
poet, playwright,
repairer, sharer
of your most secret
self.

& what are you
to me?
Son & brother
that I never
had—
clandestine Claudius,
hamstrung Hamlet,
mescaline Malvolvio?

What I want
to tell you

is that
I love you.

Impermanent
as we are,
may you
love me.

The Fork to Take

I had pegged you as
protégé, adoptee,
someone I could save.

The last thing
I needed
was
another lover.

You call yourself
"an accident
looking
for a place
to happen."
I call you
my sweet, my love,
not only
because you carry knives
for me
& want to beat up
all my
ex-husbands—
but because
you can laugh
at yourself
for wanting to.

We dream
of the baby
we will never have.
The little Jewish WASP
with golden blue eyes,
poems on the tip of his tongue,

your height, my hair,
& jokes that hit
their targets
on a slant.

He will never be
in the Social Register.
But will he know
which fork to take—
as you did
when you drove
off my road,
slyly taking the wrong fork
in order to stay
the night?

O you are sly,
my sweet wheat
looking for
a harvest.

Shall I reap you?
Shall I do to you
what the hurricane
does with the waving
grain?
Shall I thresh & bind you,
run barefoot
through your body
trying to stamp out
death?

Or shall I merely
let you
lift me up

like the wind spinning
an errant seed,

& let it
take me
where it will,
right fork,
wrong fork,
no fork
at all,
since we will take
the same path
through
the air
after all?

Toward Life

I did not stop
marching toward life.
—NERUDA

Wounded as I was—
by the madmen,
the daft Hamlets with poems
in their hair,
the chill men who wanted
to fuck their way
into my warmth
& leave me
cold,
the half-baked
novelists, the doctors
who could not heal
themselves,
the actors
who could not remember
their lines,
the professors
I had to teach;
all the Persons
from Porlock
invading the heart
of my poem—
I did not stop
marching toward
love;
I did not seal off
my heart.

& then you appeared—
suddenly,
unexpectedly—
as life is always
unexpected.
The new baby
arriving
in the same radiance—
an ordinary face
suddenly turning
extraordinary—
eyes, nose, mouth
suddenly
indispensable,
suddenly
beautiful
beyond
explanation,
suddenly necessary
as rain.

Because
I did not stop marching,
because
I never let the scar tissue
form,
because
my heart is open
to ache,
because
my legs will twine
around a new lover
& mean it
(as if love could last)—
you
marched into my life.

You marched in
sloping in to the wind,
your hair combed
as if with a fork,
your face sweet & open
as a puppy's
& as starving for love & for warmth
as a Dickens hero.

O my Pip,
my Oliver,
my Copperfield—
how I want to hold you
& make it all
all right.

Let me march
toward life
before you.
There is nothing to fear
but

stopping.

When I Am an Old Lady

When I am an old lady
the young men
will come to me
& sit trembling
at my trembling
feet
saying:

you must have been
beautiful
when you were young;
you must have been
a wonderful lover—
& perhaps
they will still feel
that current
which you say
passes from me
to you
& which you give back
doubled
on our wild
afternoons.

The madness
will still be there—
the current of sex,
of poetry, of heroism—
which is only
another name
for God
passing through us—

God, Goddess,
whoever
we call Her—

that ancient lady
who sits above the world
spinning out
our destinies.

She looped your life
around mine;
she took the weft
of your need
& gave me
the bright threads
to weave you
into my life—

old Circe
playing music on her loom,
& weaving men
into her glittering
tapestry.

Woven into her cloth,
still,
they feel free.
Bewitched by her poems,
still,
they feel strong.
Drunk on her Pramnian wine,
still,
they feel clear—
as if they were marching
through life
alone.

But it is she
who guides them,
leading them
now by their cocks,
now by their hearts,
now by their swinishness—

but what does *she* feel
alone
on her cloud throne?
She feels lonely.
Lonely to know
all she knows
& lonely even being loved
by so many

sleepy
beasts.

For C. . . . concerning Blake

Man has no Body distinct from his Soul; for that call'd
Body is a portion of Soul discern'd by the five Senses,
the chief inlets of Soul in this age. . . . Energy is the
only life, and is from the Body; and Reason is the
bound or outward circumference of Energy. . . .
Energy is Eternal Delight. . . . Those who restrain
desire, do so because theirs is weak enough to be
restrained; and the restrainer or reason usurps its
place & governs the unwilling. . . . And being
restrain'd, it by degrees becomes passive, till it is only
the shadow of desire . . .
—WILLIAM BLAKE
The Marriage of Heaven and Hell

Ripe for rebellion,
& with no
backwards gears
in your car,
you race
into your
life,
knowing that
energy
is eternal delight,
& that only those
who love
with the pure hilarity
of gods or clowns
will be saved.

O you know
that hilarity
is a serious
business,

& you know
that snow
& blood
are no
opposites.
I know it, too.
It is the knowledge
that binds
us,

the current
that passes
from hip to hip,
the bond we make
with lip
& tongue.

Fortyish men
hesitate,
want to be loved
for themselves
alone,
refuse to be
"sex objects."

It is
the virgin girl
of the '50s
now speaking
through the male
mouth.

But you know
that sex & soul
are no opposites
& that virginity

has nothing to do
with the matter.

Pure, unspoiled
priapic maniac—
you are racing
your motor,
racing your five
senses,
testing
Blake's theorems
with eye & tongue,
lip & finger,
unrestrained desire.

Desire is its
own reward.
It propels the poem
as if the penis
were a pen,
& that pen
propelled
by rocket fire.

Reason will never
usurp
your soul;
reason will never
take you.

Ransomed by blood,
exiled
by your own
lack of
backwardness,

your lack
of guile & gear—

the inlets
of your soul
are open;
the pattern
of your life
is clear.

No shadow
across
your desire,
& your desire
no shadow.

O let us
read Blake
together
& rejoice—

& then
let us open
the windows
of the senses

& let the light
shine
in.

I Try to Keep

I try to keep
falling in love
if only to keep
death

at bay.

I know
that the burned
witches,
that the seared flesh
of the enemy—

O we are all
each other's
enemies,
even sometimes those
who lately
were

lovers—

are not
to be reconstituted
nor healed

by my
falling
in love;

& yet
here is
the paradox:

love drives
the poem—

& the poem
is
hope.

To the Muse

... poetry wakes in me; my soul,
Gripped by a lyrical excitement, trembles ...
The monster's moving and it cleaves the deep ...
It sails. Where shall we sail? ...
—PUSHKIN
Autumn, A Fragment
translated by D. M. Thomas

Is it the power of poetry
or the power of sex?
All morning a coal
burned in my gut
till I could talk
to you,
a hot coal of desire
singeing my lungs,
a hot coal bursting
with unwritten poems.

I read Pushkin,
who also knew
how desire drives
poetry
& poetry drives
desire.
Pimping for poetry,
I fall in love,
become
my own procuress
to the muse.

& who is he?
A character

I have created?
Blue-eyed, loitering
in a black tuxedo,
black tie, black thoughts
on snowy nights,
tucked rows
of starchy shirt
& no trousers,
hard-on pointing
at the sky?

I was wearing
black tie, too—
but nothing else—
& crying
for the muse
to fill me
full of poetry.
I bit his neck
as all the poems
spurted out
& blood & semen flowed.

Red rose, white rose.
Our love
is a Shakespearian
history play—
all Lancaster & York—
bloody snow,
snowy blood,
poetry
& screams that pierce
the dark.

We dream, of course,
of sailing

in "the Sugar Isles"
—as 18th century pyrates
called them—
of waking up together
in the deep,
of the short
but dream-filled nights
aboard a sloop. . . .

The boat rocks;
the coffin of the deep
becomes the cradle
of our curious love.
I lick the salty tears
from your sweet skin;
your body is
my salt lick,
& your eyes
the very ocean
in which
I swim.

You cleave the deep
in search
of your own
poetry,
you probe the bottom
of the mystery.

Muse to me
as I am muse
to you—
we sail,
we sail,
we sail—
where shall we sail?

Love's Abattoir

Why does your love
make me feel I dwell
in a cathedral of entrails,
a sort of abattoir
of passions bloody
as the dawn,
a fixed address of death tested
& tested again,
& stared down,
an address of death beaten,
beaten into the gold
of golden cups,
cups brimming with blood,
with internal organs
still pulsing
like the gills
of undrowned fish?

Is it because
you came to me in winter
promising spring—
a spring of blood pumping,
green blood in the leaves
of the tender trees,
brown blood in their gnarled roots,
crystal blood in the glazed reservoir,
blood that is brutal
though it sings?

Or does it sing only because
it knows its own
brutality? Does it choose

singing over shrieking?
Does it drain the veins
of fire only to dowse
the blazing heart
in blood? Does it sing
its bloodsong
over the mouths of dust?

O mouths of dust—
we shall sing with you
soon enough!
O dried eyes—
we shall unsee
what you unsee!
O hearts that do not ache,
that do not bleed,
that do not pump or pulse,
we shall join your stillness
before long!

Under the green earth,
under the sea smoky blue
as the skins of whales—
but shuddering with scales
of light—
under the volcanoes
of the deep,
a rapture rises redly,
a rubicund flood
of tears, of juices,
the mixed plasmas
of life:

green for the spring,
crystal for the snows

that brought you to me,
& red, red, red
like our bloody
love.

Feeling Death

"I love you so much
I feel death,"
you said.

It's always the way
with love—
the scent of death
that clings
like ivy
to a crumbling wall.

At your age
Keats was dead,
at my age
Pushkin
had already
breathed
his last—
two years gone
but prophesying
immortality
from beyond
the grave.

Our arms
unclasp
but you go
into my bones
like nuclear fallout
into rainwater,
into my blood
like carbon

monoxide,
into my eyes
like the last flash
of blinding light
before the end.

You imagine us
standing on line
before the inquisitors.
Jews burned,
WASPs spared—
but you
walk through the fire
with me.

Or else
we are on an island
as the bomb
devours the world:
you, me, my daughter
& the dog
outlasting Purgatory,
outsmarting Hell,
because we love
each other.

Fire & brimstone cling
to our strange love.
In bed, we burn
like planets turned
to suns.

Death's in the cock,
the can, the car,
the barrel of the gun;

death's in the air;
the air
is bright
with blood.

Inventing My Life

Inventing my life
again every day
I am exhilarated,
exhausted,
in love,
in rage,
full of hate
& shaking
as a weeping birch
over a stream.

I have two loves
or three—
adding up
to none—

I, a woman
who gives her love
utterly
except for the part
I save
for the insubstantial
page,
a piece of parchment
heart
I bleed on,
a tampon
to the muse's
womb.

& you
my lover,
my impossible dreamer,

my playmate,
my blue-eyed fantasy,
my boy,
my friend,
my gruff growler,
my firm fucker,
my lovely licker,
my questioning kisser
with the curled tongue
& the interrogative
penis—

how can I ask you
to stay
here
wrapped in the dark
inside me
like a folded
rose?

You thrust
through the world,
battering your head
against death
like a baby
struggling
to be born.

You plow
through the world—
adventurer, pirate,
vagabond, lost boy
looking for the
never-never land
of your mother's
breast,

melting the snows
of her belly
with your burning
cock,
melting my heart
until it drips
upon this page.

I give birth
to you,
& you midwife
my poems.

We will not be
lifetime travellers.

Inventing my life
through you,
I also invent
my death.

O chip of my heart,
O splinter of my soul—
let us celebrate
the rites of spring
again—

before the seasons
change.

In the Whitmanic Ocean

The Whitmanic ocean
murmurs
death, death, death—
& we murmur
death,
locked within
our blissed
kisses,
locked within
our blazing
bed—
belly to belly,
our navels
whisper
death—
while our hearts
hiss
life, life, life,
& our souls
ascend—
Eros on the wings
of Thanatos. . . .

Thanateros,
my love,
my gladiator,
my swashbuckling
bloody boy—
your love feeds
on itself
like flame—
blueing at the base
& orange where

it marries
air. . . .

Are we in love
with forgetfulness—
the ease
with which
a forest turns to
air,
taking
a dozen
woodland species
to its ashen
bed?

O wedding guest
at the funeral!
O lover
whose merest kiss
is an obsession—
let me kindle
& rekindle
your heart;
let me set fire
even
to the sweat
that drips
from your chest
in sleep;
let me burn
the bridges
of your thighs
& extinguish
the flames
of your belly.

The ocean whispers
death,
but I whisper
poetry,
& I praise love
that is in lust
with death
& death
that lusts for
love
as if it were
a branch
of its dark
tree.

"No more
pessimistic poems!"
you said.
Therefore, I praise.

I praise love
that is in love
with death;
& death I praise
before

it praises
me.

The Poet Says "Never"

Fuck the future.
—MARGARET ATWOOD

I read my poems
to you.

The most frequent
word
in them
is: "never."

Never, never, never, never, never.
I am younger
than King Lear
yet already share
his philosophy.

& what are
all these "nevers"?
Protective magic?
A secret way
of saying
"always"?
A wish
to make you
fill me up
with promises
of love?

Teleological wretch
that I am—
I want to say

"always,"
so I say
"never."

Always
is never
forever.

In the beginning
is
the end.

But in
the end
is also
the beginning.

We live
balanced
on a ledge
called "now,"
over
a chasm
called "then,"
below
a sky
called "when."

When will
"when" come?

We hope
soon.

Meanwhile
we fiddle with our

nevers—
never believing
for a second
that
denying
our wish
for permanent,
possible
love
will work.

Endings
will come
when they must—
or not.

& all our *nevers*
will not drain them
of their
sharp, peculiar
pain—
nor drain
beginnings
of their
special, heedless
joy.

The bridge
between
these curious two
is: "never."

The poet walks
this bridge.

She whistles
in the dark.

Straw in the Fire

Straw in the fire,
our love is
straw in the fire—

not the straw
that the miller's daughter
spun into gold,
nor the straw
of the thatched roofs
of Hampshire,
nor the straw tossed
in the streets
when someone lay dying
of plague—
but two bodies
igniting
one need
until the very bed—
that pallet of sexual straw—
goes up
in a blaze,
taking playmates,
fantasy, folly,
& even wisdom
along.

O my lover,
my curious muse,
my mirage
in the winding
wet road—
we played

like flames
licking the wind.
We spoke
like the forked flame
in Dante's *Inferno*.

We made love
& poems,
with the sure, swift stab
of pleasure
unleashed to kill
& kill
again.

But one does not
live in poems
nor in bed.

The muse
cannot be tamed
into a drowsy
husband, lolling
on a sunny
beach.

He wings down
like Icarus
falling into the sea.
He flies like Satan
up to Heaven's Gate,
then reels
backward,
flaming his way
into Hell.

My darling
I love you,
but I never forget
that you write
your love letters
in pencil.

Time has not
revised you;
the galleys of
your brow
are unmarked by
any editor.

I kiss your joy
as it flies;
I hope to live
—like Blake—
in Eternity's
sunrise.

Twelve Days without You

Back in the USSR
You don't know how lucky you are.
—THE BEATLES

In the Odessa market,
the women stand
like wrinkled monuments
weighing out
their buckets
of sour cherries.

The onion domes
glitter in the blue sky;
the Black Sea
bobs
with corpulent tourists,
who have been eating
blini since the end
of the war.

Even the women
well past bearing
are bearing bellies
full of borscht.

& you my darling,
my dangerous shaygets,
my sweet rascal,
what do you think of
my having come
to this old country
in search of

a dead man
when I have
such a lively man
at home?

This is the final
mourning
for my grandfather—
that damned old Russian Jew
with his melancholia,
& his sad Russian songs,
& his dark paintings,
& his fear,
his fear, his fear.

I come back
to Odessa
to know
there is no going back.

The dead
are dead.

What lives of them
we bear within—
as those fat Russian women bear
their four decades
of blini.

I am as Russian
in my soul
as Pushkin—
yet as American
as Emily Dickinson.

I am finally as Russian
as you, my love—

there is
no going
back.

The poets
all over the world
know that exile
is home
& home is
a sort of exile.

Perhaps the music
we make
from hip to hip
is more hysterical
& rich
for being borne
from Jew to WASP
from WASP to Jew.

But it is, after all,
the music
of the spheres—
& our genitals
are nothing but
the lyre.

Fuck all our
ancestors!

Let them lie buried
in Odessa,
in Kiev, in Minsk,

in Virginia
& in goddamned
Darien.

We are, at least,
alive.

I wept over
the bones of the dead
at Babi Yar,
but when a little child
toddled
over the green, green grass
(greener for all the bones & blood
that fertilized
the soil),
I thought of you
& how I would like
to fuck like mad
over the dead
at Babi Yar.

Blasphemy
or holiness?
Who's to say?

History is hideous
& we are swept
into it
as with
an old twig broom
wielded by a Russian hag.

But I am done
with this mourning
my darling.

& done
with this dolorous
history.
I start anew
with you.

I bless my grandfather
for having fled
this country
of wrinkled women,
& the pervasive smell
of mildew & of sea.

I bless your grandfather,
for whatever he did
to bring you
to me.

But most of all
I want to be
your refuge
in the exile
which all of us
share.

In Venice Again with You

In this great ghost of cities,
the dreams rise
from the murky lagoon
& you dream
you kill your father
& I dream again
of my bad reviews.

A dagger hovers
in the air—
or can it be a pen?

The ghosts
are restless.

Lord Byron limps
across the Grand Canal
walking on the water.

The doges mumble
in their baths of blood;
& Tintoretto, painting, painting,
asks: "What matter
if I paint a Christ
or a satyr
as long as the chiaroscuro
is mine, all mine?"

At San Marco
the pickpockets dance,
fluttering stolen bills
like New Year's Eve
confetti.

& all the old assassins
from the past
dash through
the alleyways
transformed into cats.

The dogs sniff history
through their muzzles
& find it stinks.

The pigeons wheel & dip
making black holes
in Turner's luminescent sky.

It is all a stage set
for our dreams
as we wheel & turn
thrashing up our pasts.

Is this why lovers
come to Venice,
city of cemeteries
& black burial boats?

To set the ghosts
to rest
& build their lives
upon the dark lagoon
of death?

O my lover,
I have walked through
the crumbling palaces
with you
promising things
history teaches

that we cannot
promise.

The ghosts
are laughing.
They leer & pronounce
dire warnings
from behind
their terrifying masks.

Are they only jealous
because we're so alive?
& because we walk
in the sun
laughing
at their warnings?

We make love
again & again
to banish them—

& they,
stripped of their bodies,
having forgotten
the joy of flesh
(& how it houses spirit
not as a mask
houses a face
but as leaves
house the tree
of life),
tell us that making love
is not enough.

It is death
they want,

not love.
It is blood
they want,
not sperm.

But I am laying bets
on love again—
at least
for now.

Temporary,
permanent,
who can say?

I cast my dice
for life.

& the ghosts
reel backward—
& are gone.

Morning Madness

Exploring each other's
depths,
that surge of connection
which makes the world
seem sane,
that exchange of spirit
in the guise of flesh,
that morning hallelujah,
that hook
to eternity. . . .

All day I bear you
between my legs,
& in my heart.
Powered by your love,
there is no hill
too high to climb,
no paragraph
I cannot write,
no hosanna
I cannot howl. . . .

Shall we wear it down
with habit?
Shall that combustible connection
become, in time, homier
than fresh bread,
nourishing but unsurprising?

O my lover
meet me in the hollow
of a red thigh,
by mountains

which resemble
spouting cocks. . . .
We will keep
the madness fresh—
the red madness
that keeps us

sane.

Nobody Believes

Nobody believes in love—
not even me.

Love is the thing
you wait
to end.

Love is the thing
that will not,
cannot work.

Love is the thing
they warn you of—
the dire parents,
the friends
with their dead
marriages,
their crushed hopes.

Nothing crushes hope
but the will to make
the heart
like rock.

That will is strong.

The rock-heart stands
when the love songs crumble,
their yellowing sheet music
kept in a drawer,
their sweet hugs & tugs
forgotten,
like the merest air

of an old New England
spring.

Spring comes again
& again,
& the rock-hearts
feel the sap rising
thinking it is sex,
thinking the glands alone
cause this tumult
to the innards,
this hidden spring,
this secret river
which is hope.

Let them put it down
to sex!

Let them say
we worship Dionysus,
Bacchus, Pan,
but not the proper
gods.

Let them have
the proper gods—
Jahweh
with his heart like rock,
Christ with his blood
& thorns,
Mammon with his stock certificates,
his rates, his rates,
his bull markets,
& his late rallies.

We are rallying
alone.
We spit our love
into the wind.

Nobody can bear
to watch
our love.

Except the muse
who smiles
& sends

these
poems.

About the Author

Erica Jong is a native New Yorker who was educated at the High School of Music & Art, Barnard College, and Columbia University's Graduate Faculties, where she received her M.A. in eighteenth-century English literature.

She won her initial reputation as a poet with her first two collections, *Fruits & Vegetables* (1971) and *Half-Lives* (1973). In 1973–74 she came to public prominence as the author of the groundbreaking novel *Fear of Flying*, one of the top ten best-sellers of the '70s. In 1977, her second novel, *How to Save Your Own Life*, also became a major international best-seller, and in 1980 she published the wholly unexpected *Fanny: Being the True History of the Adventures of Fanny Hackabout-Jones*, a mock eighteenth-century picaresque novel about the exploits of a female Tom Jones.

In 1975 Jong published her third volume of poems, *Loveroot*, and in 1979 her fourth, *At the Edge of the Body*. In 1981, she again departed from the predictable with *Witches*—a study in prose and poetry of the mythic figure of the witch. Her work has been translated into more than twenty foreign languages.

Erica Jong is the mother of a young daughter, Molly Miranda, born in 1978. Since 1976, she has made her home in Connecticut.